The Incredible Shrinking LUNCHROOM

Michal Babay

Illustrated by Paula Cohen

ini Charlesbridge

Parley Elementary had the noisiest, most cluttered lunchroom in town. It was quite possibly the noisiest, most cluttered lunchroom in the entire world.

Students spent their lunchtime shouting and looking for a place to sit, instead of eating.

Finally they'd had enough.

The students wrote their principal a letter asking for help.

Dear Ms. Mensch,

Our lunchroom is too crowded and loud. There's stuff everywhere. Plus, during lunch the drama club practices and the music club sings. We can't hear each other at all!

What should we do?

Sincerely,

Your students

The principal liked her students and wanted to make them happy. She sipped coffee and thought about the letter. *Sip, think. Think, sip.*

The next morning she made an announcement over the loudspeaker.

Please take your science projects to the lunchroom. They will be displayed on tables around the room.

Now there was **even less** space for the students during lunch!

They had to turn sideways to squeeze between tables with science projects sticking out everywhere.

Food spilled. Feet slipped.

Tempers flared.

Juice was used inappropriately.

The lunchroom felt noisier and more disorganized every day.

After some time the students wrote another letter.

Dear Ms. Mensch,

Our lunchroom is louder and more squished than ever. It's a disaster!

We barely have space to eat, and we keep knocking over science projects.

This is horrible! What can we do?

Sincerely,

Your students

The principal chewed a sandwich and listened to her pet frogs croak. *Chew, listen. Listen, chew.*

The next morning she made an announcement over the loudspeaker.

A snake escaped and slithered around the water fountains.

Tarantulas molted,

hamsters squeaked,

and the worms looked confusingly like spaghetti.

The students at Parley Elementary were very unhappy. They wrote many notes to the principal.

This is the messiest mess EVER.

A hamster ate my homework.

Somebody sat on our dragon.

 The frogs are louder than my uncle when he snores.

Tell the fifth graders that pineapples are not weapons.

Ms. Mensch crunched an apple while reading
the notes. *Crunch, read. Read, crunch.*

The next morning she made an announcement over the loudspeaker.

It's dangerously hot outside. Until this heat wave breaks, all sports teams will practice in the lunchroom.

Balls flew, rackets swung, feet kicked, and whistles blew. Science projects exploded.

A snake slept on warm pizza, hamsters ate napkins,
and the tarantulas had disappeared!

The entire lunchroom stank of dirty feet and
rotten fruit.

Parley Elementary's lunchroom was now **a total** nightmare.

Student letters covered the principal's desk.

The garbage dump smells better than this.

I had to sit on a dragon.

It's so loud I can't hear my kazoo anymore.

A football squished my sandwich.

Tell the fourth graders that carrots are not swords.

I'll bring the tarantulas back soon.

This is worse than worse.

That afternoon the students enjoyed their best lunch period ever. The lunchroom felt quiet, calm, and roomy. Everyone had space to sit and spread out their lunch.

They laughed and told jokes.
There was no fighting or yelling.
Juice was used appropriately.

The next day the principal's mailbox was stuffed with chocolate and notes. She ate the chocolate, read the notes, and smiled.

The lunchroom is the best room in the whole school.

There's so much space now!

We love the lunchroom. It's so peaceful.

Thank you for the tarantulas—they were very helpful.

The Incredible Shrinking Lunchroom is my way of saying thank you to a story that influenced my entire life. In the original Yiddish folktale, popularized by Margot Zemach's classic book *It Could Always Be Worse*, a poor farmer and his family live together in a tiny house. Life is chaotic, loud—and very crowded. The farmer asks his wise rabbi for advice on how to handle this difficult situation.

Over the next few weeks, the beloved rabbi instructs the family to bring a horse, goat, cow, and chickens into their house. The hut becomes even more chaotic, loud, and crowded! Finally, the rabbi tells the farmer to put all the animals back outside, and the family delights in their quiet, spacious home. Although their hut remains as small and crowded as it was at the beginning, the family's perspective has changed so much that their home now feels wonderfully roomy and peaceful.

When I was growing up, my parents encouraged me to both reach for the stars and be grateful for what we have. They taught us that gratitude and a positive perspective would see us through difficult life situations. Because no matter how hard it felt in the moment, things could always be worse.

My hope is to share this timeless Jewish wisdom of sameach b'chelko (being content with what you have) with my readers. As a former elementary school teacher, I purposefully set my retelling of this folktale in an overcrowded school because that, unfortunately, is our modern reality. Schools have more students than space and less money than needed—and teachers work twenty-five hours a day. I fervently hope that this changes one day soon. In the meantime, let's take a moment to celebrate educators. These amazing people are experts at advocating for change, being resourceful, and inspiring students to shift their perspective.

In Yiddish, the word *mensch* refers to a kind and conscientious person, a person who acts with integrity and honor. Although at first glance it seems that Ms. Mensch is making the situation harder, in reality she is showing her students how adopting a new frame of mind changes everything. By the end of the story, their same lunchroom that felt teeny tiny now feels absolutely perfect!

Has there been a time in your life when you had to change your perspective? Congratulations! You are a mensch, too!

Thank you to my amazing parents . . . for everything. I love you.—M. B.

For Joshua and Julian, who are used to eating in messy rooms.—P. C.

Text copyright © 2022 by Michal Babay
Illustrations copyright © 2022 by Paula Cohen
All rights reserved, including the right of reproduction in whole
or in part in any form. Charlesbridge and colophon are registered
trademarks of Charlesbridge Publishing, Inc.

At the time of publication, all URLs printed in this book were
accurate and active. Charlesbridge, the author, and the illustrator
are not responsible for the content or accessibility of any website.

Published by Charlesbridge
9 Galen Street, Watertown, MA 02472
(617) 926-0329
www.charlesbridge.com

Printed in China
(hc) 10 9 8 7 6 5 4 3 2 1

Illustrations done digitally in Procreate on an iPad
Display type set in Billy Serif by David Buck/SparkyType
Text type set in Helenita Book by Rodrigo Araya Salas
Color separations and printing by 1010 Printing International
    Limited in Huizhou, Guangdong, China
Production supervision by Jennifer Most Delaney
Designed by Cathleen Schaad

Library of Congress Cataloging-in-Publication Data
Names: Babay, Michal, author. | Cohen, Paula (Illustrator),
    illustrator.
Title: The incredible shrinking lunchroom /
    Michal Babay; illustrated by Paula Cohen.
Description: Watertown, MA: Charlesbridge, [2022] | Based
    on the Yiddish folk tale retold by Margot Zemach under
    title: It could always be worse. | Audience: Ages 5–8. |
    Audience: Grades K–1. | Summary: "What do you do when
    the school lunchroom gets too crowded? The principal
    devises a clever plan to show the students how to appreciate
    what they have, shift their perspective, and use their space
    more effectively in this modern retelling of a classic Yiddish
    folktale."—Provided by publisher.
Identifiers: LCCN 2021013826 (print) | LCCN 2021013827
    (ebook) | ISBN 9781623542948 (hardcover) | ISBN
    9781632899309 (ebook)
Subjects: LCSH: School lunchrooms, cafeterias, etc.—Juvenile
    fiction. | School principals—Juvenile fiction. | Elementary
    schools—Juvenile fiction. | Tales. | Humorous stories. |
    CYAC: School lunchrooms, cafeterias, etc.—Fiction. |
    School principals—Fiction. | Schools—Fiction. | Perspective
    (Philosophy)—Fiction. | Humorous stories. | LCGFT: Folk
    literature. | Humorous fiction.
Classification: LCC PZ7.1.B116 In 2022 (print) | LCC
    PZ7.1.B116 (ebook) | DDC [E]—dc23
LC record available at https://lccn.loc.gov/2021013826
LC ebook record available at https://lccn.loc.gov/2021013827